Bicycle Bear Rides Again

by Michaela Muntean
pictures by Doug Cushman

Parents Magazine Press • New York

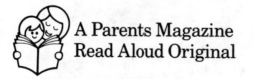
A Parents Magazine
Read Aloud Original

Library of Congress Cataloging-in-Publication Data

Muntean, Michaela.
Bicycle Bear rides again/by Michaela Muntean; pictures by Doug
Cushman.
     p.   cm.
Summary: When his uncle Bicycle Bear takes a vacation, Trike Bear
attempts to take over his delivery job and finds it more difficult
than he had thought.
ISBN 0-8193-1193-6
[1. Bears—Fiction.   2. Delivery of goods—Fiction.   3. Bicycles
and bicycling—Fiction.   4. Uncles—Fiction.   5. Stories in rhyme.]
I. Cushman, Doug, ill.   II. Title.
PZ8.3.M89Bk   1989
[E]—dc20   89-27823   CIP   AC

A Parents Magazine Read Aloud Original
Text copyright © 1989 by Michaela Muntean.
Illustrations copyright © 1989 by Doug Cushman.
All rights reserved.
Printed in the United States of America.
10 9 8 7 6 5 4 3 2 1

For Alexia, Paul,
and Colleen—M.M.

To Stephen—D.C.

"You can name any place,
Any place that you like—
I have been there and back
On the seat of a bike.

"From Peking to Paris,
From Sweden to Spain,
I have pedaled this world
Through snowstorms and rain."

"Through the darkest of nights,
Through the sun's strongest glare,
"I'm the one that you've called.
I am Bicycle Bear!

"I've delivered whatever
You've wanted to send
To your mother, your brother,
Your aunt, or a friend."

"But now winters seem longer.
(Are they getting colder?)
Or maybe it's just
That I'm getting older.

"There's a crick in my back.
There are creaks in my knees.
I would like to be warmed
By a tropical breeze."

"But who would take over?
Who would get the jobs done,
If I went away
To sit in the sun?"

He was puzzling and pedaling
Through that cold wintry air,
When along came his nephew,
Young Tricycle Bear.

Now Trike always asked
If he could help out,
For he dreamed that one day
He would have his own route.

"It's so good to see you!"
Said Bicycle Bear.
"For I was just thinking
Of going somewhere.

"But I would not feel right
About leaving town.
I'd worry that I'd let
My customers down."

"I'll take over," said Trike,
"While you get your rest.
If only you'd let me,
Why, I'd do my best!"

They quickly agreed,
Then set off for the station
So Bicycle Bear
Could start his vacation.

Trike went right to work,
But it really was rough.
The snow and the ice
Made delivering tough.

At the end of the day
He fell into his chair.
All the work he had done
Made him one tired bear.

The very next morning
Came a call from a mouse.
He wanted to know:
Could Trike move his house?

"No problem," said Trike,
"That should be a snap.
The house of a mouse
Could fit in my lap!"

If that had been true,
All would have been fine,
But that little mouse's family...

...Numbered ninety-nine!

The house had sixteen stories,
With two hundred and twenty rooms.
They were filled with cheese and chairs,
And blankets, beds, and brooms.

"I'm not sure how to do this.
But I'll *try*," said Tricycle Bear.
"The snow's too deep to pull this house.
Perhaps I'll float it through the air!"

So he went to get balloons.
He got four-hundred and four.
He tied them to the rooftop,
To the windows and the door.

"If this works," said Trike,
"This move will be a cinch."
But that house just would not budge.
No, it would not move an inch.

"Now what?" cried Trike.
"My life was going fine,
Until I met this family
That numbers ninety-nine!"

He sat down on his tricycle
To try and think things through.
He needed help to move this house.
He knew what he had to do.

He called his Uncle Bike,
Who said he'd be right there.
"I've failed you," said young Trike.
"I'm *not* a delivery bear!"

"Fiddle-dee-sticks," said Bicycle Bear.
"We'll do what must be done.
You know," he added thoughtfully,
"Two heads are better than one."

So Trike went to the station
To meet his uncle's train.
With two bears on the job,
The answer was soon plain.

"We will move this mouse's house.
We'll deliver it with ease.
All we need," said Bicycle Bear...

"...Is a great big pair of skis!"

They set off down the hill
Through the snow and ice.
They delivered that big house
And ninety-nine small mice!

"I have ruined your vacation.
I'm sorry," said Tricycle Bear.
But his uncle only laughed and said,
"I really do not care!

"I now know what I needed
Was not to sit in the sun.

"When delivering's in your blood,
Your work is what is fun.

"What I really need is help.
I could use someone like you.
Because," said Bicycle Bear,

"Five wheels are better than two!"

About the Author

MICHAELA MUNTEAN is the author of many popular books for children, including *Bicycle Bear.*

"Bicycle Bear is one of my favorite characters. As soon as I finished writing the first book about him, I knew I wanted to write another," says Ms. Muntean. "And I have lots of wonderful nieces and nephews, so I decided that Bicycle Bear should have a niece or nephew, too."

Ms. Muntean, her husband, and three dogs live in a big, old house on Long Island.

About the Artist

DOUG CUSHMAN is the illustrator of many children's books, including *Bicycle Bear.*

Mr. Cushman says he really enjoyed working on this new story. "Drawing that long sandwich was fun," he says, "because I like to eat good food. But I never ate anything that big and I don't think I could. If I had a sandwich that long, I would share it with a lot of friends."

Mr. Cushman lives in Connecticut. In addition to illustrating, he enjoys writing, cooking and playing tennis.